The Grey Dancer

Annie Latto would never forget the summer she turned eleven. There was the Coronation of the Queen, her dad's new job building the dam in the glen, and her repeated confrontations with the surly headmaster Black Alistair.

But above all it is her meeting with Lal, the young stranger who comes to live in her Highland glen, that most fascinates her. Spellbound by his mysterious story of love and injustice long ago, Annie is soon immersed in a dramatic series of events as past and present fuse into a stirring Midsummer's Eve climax, but not before she has begun to gain an awakening awareness of the challenge of life and truth.

Some other titles in Fontana Lions

THE HAUNTING OF CASSIE PALMER *Vivien Alcock*

THE STARS ARE UPSIDE DOWN *Gabriel Alington*

THE EYES OF THE AMARYLLIS *Natalie Babbit*

TIG'S CRIME *T.R. Burch*

GOOD-BYE DAY *Olive Dehn*

THE STONE BOOK *Alan Garner*

TOM FOBBLE'S DAY *Alan Garner*

GRANNY REARDUN *Alan Garner*

THE AIMER GATE *Alan Garner*

A DARK HORN BLOWING *Dahlov Ipcar*

WHEN HITLER STOLE PINK RABBIT *Judith Kerr*

THE LION, THE WITCH AND THE WARDROBE
and further six titles
in the Chronicles of Narnia by C.S. Lewis

ALBESON AND THE GERMANS *Jan Needle*

THE SIZE SPIES *Jan Needle*

THE TREE THAT SAT DOWN *Beverly Nichols*

THE SILVER CROWN *Robert O'Brien*

WHEN MARNIE WAS THERE *Joan Robinson*

PLACE MILL *Barbara Softly*

ALISON FELL

The Grey Dancer

Fontana · Lions

First published in Great Britain 1981
by William Collins Sons & Co Ltd
First published in Fontana Lions May 1982
by William Collins Sons & Co Ltd
14 St James's Place, London SW1

© Alison Fell 1981

Printed in Great Britain by
William Collins Sons & Co Ltd, Glasgow

For Ivan and Zim

The year Annie Latto turned eleven was a year of queer weather. It was during that winter her father stretched out his arm and pointed down the valley at the fireballs that jumped and played like red balloons along the snowdrifts, and the thunder clapped over the golden eagle's nest on Bohespic Hill, until Annie feared for the bird – which indeed was not seen all the long spring.

Summer came late and burning, so that the mud of the quarrying at Laggan dried to pale dust and blew up the valley when the wind turned westerly, misting the surface of the river pools and dulling the shine of the bramble leaves, and school days in the black granite house by the waterfall were drear beyond bearing. It was as if the weather had curdled the Dominie's temper too – not that his was ever the sweetest, but as the weeks and the lessons trailed by, his black-coated arm reached more often for the tawse, and the strokes came down harder. So it went on, until not even the bravest in the class could stop the tears seeping out from the bite of the

7

leather beast, and Annie's nerves were stretched tight through every lesson. It was during that summer they dubbed him Black Alistair.

But there were strokes of luck, too, for Annie and the others at Crianoch. First, there was the new queen being crowned, and her Coronation day brought a new thing into the schoolhouse. It was a television, the first to be seen in the village, which Black Alistair had hired to let them all see Westminster Abbey and the young queen with her heavy crown, and the Earls and Duchesses bowing their ermine to the stone floor as she passed by. It took a long time. For hour upon hour Annie peered at the flickering grey square. Organs played, and at the end Annie nearly cried when the queen came past in her Cinderella carriage waving so sadly, and she worried what would happen if the queen needed to go to the bathroom in the middle of it all.

The other good thing was that after Annie's dad got a job on the hydroelectric scheme at Laggan, where the new dam was going up, a new man came to take his place driving the school bus from Laggan to Crianoch.

The new man was a stranger to the valley, a gypsy, some said, who had come wandering with the tinkers over Rannoch Moor from Moidart or even the Isle of Skye. Lachlan McLennan was the name he went by in the village, but from the start to the young ones he was Lal.

"Lal? Aye, a real tink's name," Alec Batty whispered loudly right behind the driver's seat.

Annie raised her fist to him, snivelling sly boy that he was, but Lal just turned and laughed.

"It's a grand lilt your sweet lips give it," he said, and caught Annie's eye.

Annie blushed and looked away, and then looked back. Never had she seen such golden eyes on a man. They were the yellow of a burn in full sun, or the feathers at the throat of an eagle.

"They're aye feared of strangers here," she said shyly, for she had to say something. "I ken, for I came here strange the same as you."

"Is that so?" said Lal, and looked at her straight and clear, as if she was a grown-up. Annie tried not to stare. Lal's eyelids were strange, too. They were the sort of lids you only see on adults after weddings or ceilidhs or some such thing – drooping, sleepy-drunk, as if with a great contentment.

"Aye, three years back," she answered.

"And where are you living?"

"Dal estate," Annie said, and sat back in her seat, for Lal's hand was on the gear stick and sliding the old green bus out on to the Laggan road.

Lal drew in his breath and said softly, "Ach, Dal, is it?"

Past the end of the loch, past Mairi McDonald's farm, past the fir forest of Murchus, along the stretch of road by the salmon ladder, Lal drove as calm and peaceful as a fisherman paddling his boat across a pool. Annie found her eyes glued to the back of his head, to the bit where his hair met his sunburned neck. The long strands there were the colour of pollen when it blows from the pine cones. Annie stared, and many thoughts and wonderings crossed her mind about this stranger who seemed to know of Dal.

Annie's hand had strayed to the back of her own neck, touching the rough bristles there, and suddenly she felt a spark of rebellion. Why must faither take me to old Batty, she thought. Why must he shave my neck with his clippers? I willnae go. Not once more.

A wasp blew in through the open window then, and swirled in the wind currents. Annie flailed as it came near her, but it came to rest on Lal's back, on his checked shirt just below the collar. It began to crawl upwards towards his hair.

"Watch, there's a wasp on ye," she said, leaning forward to speak into his ear. "Dinnae move, though. I'll have it off."

Lal whistled softly and drove on. With her spelling book from her satchel Annie stole up on the insect, stalked it, then batted it, and tried to get it back out the window. It hung in the wind for a minute, then fell back inside, where Annie could not see it, but could hear its angry buzzing.

"Thanks, lass," Lal said, just as Annie was beginning to feel embarrassed at the fuss she'd made. She bent down to see what was crawling on her leg just as the sting went into her calf. She yelped like a pup.

"Annie's stung, Annie's stung!" It was Alec Batty, shouting and jumping up and down beside her.

"Wheesht," she hissed. "You shouldnae distract a driver's attention." It came out, just like that, in the words her father had used again and again.

"What's that?" Lal looked over his shoulder at Annie, who had pulled her leg up and was bent over looking at the sting.

"The wasp got her."

Lal slowed the bus and pulled it in to the side of the road. Annie felt her face blush as red as a rosehip.

"Dinnae mind, Mr McLennan," she said quickly. "I'll spit on it," and she began to dab spit on the wound as if her life depended on it.

"Lal is how I'm called," he said gravely, and hoisted her up in his arms, and set her down on a boulder at the roadside.

"Wait here, now." He took the sheep fence at one leap, while Annie sat there holding her leg in one hand. With the other hand she pulled her hair over her face to shield it from the children who gawped and giggled from the bus at all this carry on.

"Who's got a crush on the tink, then?" screeched Sandy McFie, with his freckled snout squashed against the glass.

Annie scowled at the window and mouthed, "Yer wee brother eats worms."

After a minute Lal returned carrying a tuft of wet moss. It smelt clean and sweet when he pressed it to her leg.

"Hold that sphagnum to it," he said, "and I'll have you home in no time."

Annie limped back to her seat.

"Mind he doesnae poison ye with his tink's tricks," Alec Batty whispered.

*   *   *

Next day at school the whole playground hummed with talk about what a daftie the new driver was, and how he'd stopped the bus to fetch a weird potion for Annie Latto's leg.

"Awa wi' ye," Annie had to keep saying. "Anybody kens sphagnum moss is a *medicine*," she'd say as scornfully as she could, although her mother had only told her the night before. "Before there were doctors and pills, it was a medicine, *everybody* kens it," she insisted. But all the same, when it was time to go home and take their Coronation mugs and wee blue bibles the Queen, it seemed, had sent to all the schools in Scotland, Annie didn't sit near Lal. Instead she sat farther back in the bus, next to Mairi McDonald, and only nodded goodbye to him when he stopped to let her off at the blackthorn hedge by the end of Dal track.

"All right now, lass?" he asked, and she told him yes.

*   *   *

12

And indeed she was all right, she thought to herself after tea, sitting alone in the birch wood with the early evening breeze rustling the branches and only her thoughts and the occasional hare for company. The birch wood crowned the highest point of the ridge of Dal, which lay in a long spur between the valleys of Crianoch and Laggan. Behind Annie the fir-clad hills of Murchus spread like a big animal, six impenetrable miles of them stretching west as far as the narrow shores of Loch Crianoch. On the southernmost point of the ridge, among smooth lawns and cedar trees, the Big House of Dal stood gloomy and splendid, overlooking the gorges where the river foamed and tumbled on its way to the lower, flatter lands of Laggan. It was the Laggan valley Annie looked out over now, a wide sweep of boulder-strewn fields cleft with burns and marsh. From the byre of the home farm the cattle, newly-milked, moved in a slow procession down the ridge, and the evening sun raised a red glow in their brown hides. Annie watched thoughtfully, stroking her leg. The sting had truly cooled, the puncture mark was gone, and the pain with it.

She leaned her head back, resting it against the trunk of the tallest tree of the wood. She had named this tree the Grey Dancer, for the way it swayed and rippled its branches higher than any other tree of Dal, and wilder. She yawned, and stretched out beneath it, raising her arms behind her head and clasping them round the papery bark of the trunk. She put her ear close to it, listening. From within came the familiar creaking and rending which had always convinced her that the tree yearned to be dancing – not just in the top branches which she could see waving and fluttering against the blue sky – but in all of it, a whole long movement which even the deep roots joined in.

Suddenly a sound of twigs breaking brought Annie out of her dream, She sat upright and alert; more twigs splintered. She jumped to her feet in time to see a glowering red face appear over the brow of the hill, and Fergie, the ghillie's son, bore down on her. She swore out loud, and turned to run, but not fast enough to escape the rough hand which grabbed her shoulder.

"Got ye!" Fergie's breath was right in her face, and all his bad teeth stared at her, so that her mind went to the row of dead buzzards and crows which hung on a hazel tree in the field to scare off vermin.

"No ye don't," Annie's knee was up and as near his belly as she could get it – for he was a tall lad, coming sixteen and lanky – and Fergie leaned off balance to avoid the blow. Catching his foot in a tree root, he loosened his hold, and Annie fled.

"Wee tink," he yelled after Annie as she flew down the hill, clearing heather clumps and fallen trees, her feet scarce touching the ground. "Yer dad's a poacher."

Annie heard his feet coming after her, crashing through the bracken, and she hoped hard that an adder would get him before he got to her. Fergie was a beast, she raged as she ran, and his father was always licking his moustache and tipping his tweed hat to the laird of Dal.

The evening sun kept up a golden flashing through the trees as Annie raced for the far fringe of the birch grove. There the trees thinned and the land sloped steeply down to a burn, and then rose again to the north, towards the shoulder of Bohespic. Annie raced and cursed, for Fergie's rush had cut her off from the path along the ridge which led home to the grey house above the farm. But if she could clear the burn, she thought, and head for the larch woods of Bohespic, she could surely lose the lad who louped so heavily behind her.

As Annie slowed to slither under a barbed wire fence, her eye caught a golden fluttering in the sky, like the flashing of the sun through the birches. She heard the surge of wings just above her head, and thought, "It's the eagle come back." She glanced behind her to see how near Fergie was, but somehow her foot caught on a trailing bramble, and her ankle went over as she fell. She felt the strap of her sandal snap as she tumbled and rolled and ended up at the bottom of a small hillock. When she tried to stand upright she found her feet were squelching in the black slime of a bog.

Fergie came down the hill grinning like a monkey.

"Look what ye've done," she yelled at him, pointing at the scratches bleeding on her legs, and her clean socks now sodden with the peat mud.

Fergie smirked. "Aye. Ye'll no tell, though. For

I'll let on to the laird that your faither's been at his trout."

"Liar," said Annie, angrily.

"And pottin' at mallards up the hill of an evening."

"Damned liar," Annie said again, but she knew the truth of it. She had been with her dad, time and time again, running to fetch the rabbit or bird as it lay dying, like a gun dog roots in the bracken clumps for the catch.

Fergie lolled on the grass beside Annie as she stripped off her wet socks. "Gie's a kiss, then," he urged, breathing in her ear like a bull.

"Get awa'," she growled, but he came in closer. "I hate ye," she muttered, scared in spite of herself. She tried to get up, but Fergie's big hand with the broken nails got her arm in a grip like a ferret's jaws, and would not be shaken off. His hairy jumper came down smothery on her face as he leaned over to pin both her arms down in the grass, and the sun disappeared behind his bulk.

But all at once another, quicker, shadow joined his; there was a beating of heavy wings, the whirr of a big bird shifting the air. Fergie cried out and fell back, clutching his right arm. In the second before Fergie took his hand away from his arm and gaped at the blood, Annie saw above her the smoulder of the eagle's golden eye, and a bird's form too long and lissom for any eagle of those parts.

A queer feeling came over her then as Fergie lay moaning beside her. It was a feeling of lightness and

16

strength, as if her bones had turned to hollow steel, and the muscles of her thin arms glowed for a minute like molten strings of glass coming off the blower's pipe. There was a ring of heat around her like a forge. The fine feeling only lasted a few moments, but it left something changed. Although Annie could never have said it to friend or foe, she knew that the eagle had left something to her. Like some kind of territory which was in her own keeping.

Fergie stirred beside her, and clenched his fist.

"Ye willnae come in," she hissed, not knowing why she spoke so, and with a swipe of her muddy sock she slapped him once across the face. His mouth gaped open in surprise, and he reeled back. His foot slipped and his trouser legs took a soaking in the bog.

"Ye'll no' tell." Now it was Annie's turn to threaten.

Fergie cowered beneath her. "I willnae, I willnae."

"And ye willnae chase me once more."

Fergie shook his head dumbly. Annie plucked a clump of sphagnum from the bog and held it out to him. "Here's medicine for the clawing you took." She laughed at his scared look. "You'll take no harm from it."

* * *

Black Alistair lived with his old mother, who was never seen outside the schoolhouse garden except for the time her chrysanths won a prize and Black Alistair wheeled her down the brae in a wheelchair to the prize giving in Crianoch Hall. Annie's mother and father were forever telling her not to make fun of the Headmaster and his mother, but that didn't stop them giggling to themselves about the night Alistair arrived at the Fancy Dress Social done up as a nurse.

"Oh aye, he was bonny," her dad had roared, and her mother had nudged him, trying to stop giggling.

"Bonnier still when he kicked up his skirt in the Gay Gordons and showed his suspenders."

"He's a poor soul, a poor soul," her mother muttered.

Puzzled, Annie had looked up from her tea. "But he belts us all the time," she said quickly, hoping her parents would listen this time. "He belts us even if we only get a spelling wrong."

"Oh aye," her mother said, as if her mind was off somewhere else. "Well, you'll deserve it, likely." Annie could see there was no more sense in saying it again than there was in wishing her jumper wasn't darned, so she finished her tea in silence and went out to sit with the hens in the yard.

"I dinnae deserve it, I do *not*," she told herself again and again. But still the doubt lingered, like a mist over a marsh, clouding and blurring everything that was sure and clear.

* * *

As the summer days slipped past, Black Alistair's mother was seen less and less bending over her herbaceous borders, and there was talk in the Co-op and the sweetie shop of a cancer which was wasting her away.

One Monday, during school dinners, the children queuing by the hatch for second helpings saw the Headmaster draw the blinds in the upstairs windows of the schoolhouse. Alec Batty rattled his knife and fork and squeaked. "There's an ambulance. Comin' up the brae."

Annie piled her dishes by the hatch and went out to the playground. Just then Black Alistair emerged from his back door. He had his hand up over his eyes, shielding them from the glare of the sun.

"Come here, Annie." He beckoned to her. She went unwillingly, for it was getting so that you never knew what wrongdoing Black Alistair could invent next. She stood in front of him quite scared, wondering what he would think of to punish her for. She tried to see the expression in his eyes, but the sun on his glasses made them invisible.

When he spoke, his voice was gruffer than usual. "Run to Lachlan McLellan's," he said. "Tell him the school is closing early, so he's to bring the bus round in half an hour."

"Yes, sir." Annie shivered. Behind the Headmaster's shoulder was the glint and splash of the waterfall by the schoolhouse. She hoped he hadn't seen her sitting there at playtime.

"He lodges over the Co-op. But you'll know that, I suppose." Black Alistair's spectacles flashed at her.

"Yes, sir, I know, sir," she stammered, "it's the same place I lived before Dal."

"Hurry up, then." He clapped his hands together, dismissing her, and turned to meet the ambulance.

Annie ran down the brae, through the back close by the Co-op, and up the outside stairs of the wooden house. She banged hard on the door, and stood sniffing the familiar creosote smell of the wood. There was no answer. Seeing the door slightly ajar, she gave it a bit of a push, and peeked in. It was all changed from when her parents had rented it, when her dad had worked in the Co-op garage. Lal had painted over the flowered wallpaper, and the room was very white, stark as snow on the moor. Even the kitchen sink surrounds were white.

There was a rug of foreign pattern on the floor by the window, with the sunbeams catching the colours – crimson, and bracken brown, and a blue dark as the night sky.

In the middle of the floor, where her mother's three-piece suite had formed a big barricade, stood a low table. It was painted with a smooth scarlet paint that Annie had seen on bicycles or cars, but never on furniture. On the table lay a knife, of the kind used for skinning deer, but smaller, with an odd-shaped handle which looked as if it had been fashioned from a white bone.

In the bedroom, a rucksack hung behind the door, and a pair of strong lacing boots were set neatly beside the narrow iron bed.

The sound of an ambulance siren from up the hill brought her back to herself with a start, and she went back to the living room, chewing her lip and wondering where to look for Lal. She was thinking maybe she'd try the garage when her eyes caught something on the wall and opened wide with surprise. Above the mantelpiece, next to a big feather, was a drawing of a tree. But it was not just any tree, it was her own tree in the birch wood, the one she called the Grey Dancer. She went closer to get a better look at it.

But just then there was a breath of wind at the door, a rustle, and Lal stood there, smiling at her.

"Aye, Annie, then. What brings you here?" The flecks of yellow in his eyes sparkled at her, his shadow was hiding the sun from her. And a thought came swimming up as sudden as a trout darts for the fly. She clapped her hand over her mouth, forgetting all about her urgent message.

"What is it, lass?" Lal took her arm. "You've turned right pale."

"It was on the moor," she blurted. "There was an eagle." She looked at the feather, and at the Grey Dancer, and her head spun. "And the tree!"

"Wheesht, lass." Lal turned suddenly stern on

her, or so she took it. The laugh went out of his eyes, and she felt the loss of it like a cold draught blowing under a door.

"Sit ye down." Lal drew her over to the old rocker by the fireplace. Taking both her hands in his, he looked at her fair and square. "No, you're no' daft," he said, answering the question in her mind. "I'll explain it all to ye, I promise." Annie nodded, blinking back tears.

"But you've a message for me, have ye no'?"

Annie took her hands back and gripped the arms of the rocker to pull herself together. "It's the bus. Mr Black says to bring it now. I think his mother's deid," she said in a rush.

Lal nodded. "I saw the blinds go down."

"The school's to close early," said Annie, feeling her strength begin to come back.

"Let's be going, then," said Lal, holding the door open.

On the doorstep Annie paused and looked back at the white room, wanting, yet not wanting, to stay in it, and then she turned and ran down the wooden stairs. At the bottom she looked back and said quickly, "But ye'll tell me?"

Lal looked down at her from the top step and put his hand across his breast, like a priest or a Red Indian. "Aye. Before the week's out."

On the way home, Annie's face burned, thinking about the way she turned brazenly and made him promise. Was it not a cheek, asking for all these things to be explained? Behaviour like that would have earned her at least a sharp word, if not a raised hand, from any adult she knew.

Lal drove, the other children chattered with excitement about their day off, and Annie sat quietly, chewing at her hair and wrestling with the waves of shame and worry.

The bus had just dropped Mairi McDonald and her wee sister when there was a commotion at the back. Annie smelt burning. She jumped up to see, and at that moment Lal must have smelt the fire too, for he slammed the brakes on so hard that she nearly fell over. He went up the aisle of the bus at a rare speed. From where she was it looked as if Sandy McFie had been playing with matches, and had set a whole matchbox exploding. The girls were shrieking and laughing, and over the din Annie heard Lal shout, "I'll no' have ye playing with matches! Fire *burns*, ye ken." He sounded just as sharp as any adult telling children off, and Annie's stomach tightened. She retreated to her seat, and didn't smile at him when he came back down the corridor grim-faced.

* * *

It turned out that Black Alistair's mother died that night in Pitlochry hospital, and the next few days at school the Headmaster did not appear. Quiet little

Miss Boyd took the infants and the older ones in the same room, so not much work was done, and mercifully there was a holiday from the noise of the blackboard pointer crashing down on the desks, and the whine of the tawse as it sliced the air. The days went by pleasantly enough, but each morning on the way to school, and each afternoon on the way back, Annie was gripped by anxiety. Lal showed no signs of talking to her, and she began to think her suspicions had been right: his promises were only to keep her quiet. But then, on the night before Mrs Black's funeral, Lal stopped the bus for a bit longer than usual at Dal track.

"I've some letters to leave in the box," he said, getting out of the bus with her. Annie saw him pretend to slip something into Dal mailbox, and meanwhile he whispered, "I havenae forgotten, Annie. Tomorrow morn, I'll meet ye by your tree. After the funeral." He looked hard at her. "Trust me." And he swung back into the bus and was away.

*　　*　　*

The day of old Mrs Black's funeral dawned bright and windy, with a sun as fierce as Perthshire ever saw, and white small clouds tearing east to west along the glen. By eleven o'clock Annie was already

24

sitting cross-legged against the bole of the Grey Dancer, although the hearse would only just be straining up Crianoch brae to the cemetery, and Lal would have to drive to Dal after that. Her mother had been off to the Big House at nine, grumbling that if she had to wash dishes at Dal, then Annie could at least offer to wash them at home. But the morning's porridge pot had been too daunting, and Annie told herself that no one could stay in the house on a day like this anyway. So she'd come out, and spent an hour perfecting the earthworks on her dam in the burn, and a short while training newts to dive off the dam into the pool, and now here she was.

Down below in the fields Fergie zigzagged, laying his snares. Annie watched him, still wary, until he vanished into the Home Farm. She sat chewing a head of clover and watched the bees fight to keep their balance against the strength of the wind while they sucked the nectar from foxglove and wild rose. On the pond by her house the family of mallards took off with a faint splash and flutter. Annie dozed, soothed by the summer sounds and the tiny groans from the Grey Dancer, until a flap of wings woke her, and she opened her eyes in a dazzle of light. It was Lal.

As he stood there grinning above her, with his checked shirt flung over his shoulder, Annie found herself all delight from head to foot. She sat up and smiled back until her face nearly split, relief and happiness rippled through her so.

"Glad I am to see something cheery this morning," Lal said. "I cannae abide funerals where there's neither a tear shed nor a laugh let be. Och, and what a day, too – the village men were all sweating in their black." He laughed, and Annie felt a bit shocked. She put her hands to her hot cheeks and looked up at him. The sun shot his hair with bronze and gold, the colour of eagle's feathers. Oh, if only she could ask, if only she could get the words out. . . .

She opened her mouth, but suddenly Lal's face turned sad. He reached out to stroke the trunk of the Grey Dancer. "Let's sit awhile, then, and I'll tell ye." He tapped the tree lightly with his finger and looked up into its branches. "The tree's an old friend, Annie. It comforts me to sit here, for it was here I did my courting with her. With Isobel." He sighed softly. "To begin with, I must tell ye of Isobel."

"You're married?" Annie was taken aback.

"In a way, lass. Not in any way your Kirkmen would accept. They wouldnae then, they wouldnae now. It was all a long time ago, Annie, afore ye were born. . . ."

Annie's neck prickled with fear. "She's not dead, though?"

"Might as well be," Lal said, with a groan, a groan the tree seemed to answer. "Might as well." And then, to Annie's horror, he let out a sob.

She thought quickly, and said, "I bet she was bonny," and felt as clumsy as Fergie. She waited, embarrassed, while Lal brushed the tears from his eyes.

"Aye," he said, "Bonny enough." "She loved this tree, you know. She told me she saw it as a dancer." He smiled. "She thought that to dance must be as near heaven as ye could get."

"But I call the tree the Grey Dancer," Annie said excitedly.

Lal smiled to himself. "I might have known it." Reaching into his pocket he pulled out the knife Annie had seen in his house and picked up a branch of ash wood. He held the branch this way and that, as if to see what shape was waiting within it, and began to whittle away with the knife. "She had a withered leg, you see. From when she was a baby." He turned to Annie. "You have a look of her, lass – she had the same red hair and the white skin.

"I'll not forget the day she came down Bohespic Hill to Laggan. From far off you could see her hair in the sun, red as rowans. She wore a green dress, I mind, and she carried a bundle on her back – spinning things, it was. As she came nearer you could see the limping. She came by the rig I was ploughing and asked me for a cup of milk, and looked straight in my eyes with such a twinkle that I blushed scarlet.

'Have ye come far?' I asked, as she sat drinking the milk I'd brought her.

'From Laidon, over the moor,' she answered. 'And from Badenoch before that.'

'You've no people, then?' I asked, but I knew the

27

answer, for many folk had lost kin in the troubles then. She said nothing, just shook her head and picked up her bundle, and I was afraid I had offended her. But she thanked me kindly enough, and set off into the village to look for lodgings."

Lal paused to pull a bit of couch grass, and sat for a moment sucking thoughtfully on the sweet white stalk. Annie's mind knotted with confusion. "But *when?*" she said, trying to think back to her history books. "I cannae understand when you're telling me about. It all sounds old and *funny.*"

Lal looked long and serious at her. "Don't be afraid, Annie, of owt I tell ye. Or of owt in the world. Can ye promise me that?"

Annie thought for a while. "No," she said honestly, "I cannae promise," and felt miserable. She sneaked a look at Lal. "I can try, though." She waited, and her stomach clenched with apprehension.

"You see, Annie, it all happened a fearsome long time ago. A hundred years and more."

A big sob tried to force its way out of Annie's mouth, and she felt her body shrink away from Lal's. Her hand went out to touch the Grey Dancer, for safety. A few feet away Lal continued carving, as ordinary as anything. She took a sidelong look at his hands; they looked real and strong enough, and young, not at all the frail hands of a ghost or a dead man. Blue veins pulsed under the skin as his fingers worked busily with the knife, and the skin itself bore the bloom of the sun. Lal turned then, and saw how she was examining him. She looked away quickly, down the valley. Dust was rising from the tunnelling on Bohespic Hill, and away down the Laggan the rim of the new dam shone white in the sun. Annie shivered.

"Here, lass." Lal smiled, laying his left hand against her cheek. It felt like her dad's, warm and slightly calloused. "See – it's as real as yourself."

Annie nodded without looking at him. She wanted badly to go. She scanned the valley road for a sight of her dad's car. If he was on early shift, he'd be starting for home now, driving through the gates of the camp, bumping over the yellow mud road rutted by heavy lorries. Was he on early? She tried to remember.

Lal made a sudden movement then, and the knife blade flashed. Annie jumped. "Bleeds as well." Lal laughed and pointed to the blood oozing from a small cut in the ball of his thumb.

Annie gaped. "You cut yourself."

"Aye," he smiled. "But you're right enough, Annie. For there's magic in it." Lal put his thumb to his mouth and sucked it. "You must hear me out before you'll understand. Will you bear with me?"

Annie bit her lip. "Aye," she said hesitantly. She hugged her knees tight to her. "But no' now. My dad'll be back." Squinting hard down the Laggan road she could nearly convince herself she saw the blue Austin through the haze. "I've got to go." She jumped up.

"Shake on it?"

Annie held out her hand gingerly. His grip was firm and reassuring and left a small streak of blood on her palm.

"Saturday. The morn's Saturday," she said, with a question in her voice.

Lal brushed his blond hair out of his eyes and looked hard at her. "So. Saturday it will be, then."

Annie turned and ran down the ridge. The van pulled into the yard just as she arrived, panting, at the house. Her dad's dirty face smiled at her from the van window. "Aye, lass, what's the excitement about?"

She smiled back with relief. "Nothing. Running, just." Inspired suddenly, she said: "I got right up by a deer, and it ran, and I raced it." The lie made her blush.

Her dad climbed out of the van. "Carry my piece-tin in, will ye?" He handed the plastic box to her and yawned widely, stretching. "Och, I've had it the day, Annie. I wish I was back on the bus. It's no weather for working the crusher."

Annie nodded in agreement as they went up the front steps. Her dad's walk was heavy and tired.

"It's no' safe, ye ken. The machines arenae maintained right. They willnae employ enough men."

Annie nodded knowledgeably, feeling very safe and warm herself next to his big overall-covered arm. He rested his hand on her head for a moment.

"They're just asking for it," he said grimly.

* * *

Annie sighed, and sweated on up the track from the home farm with the eggs in a paper bag and the milk slapping at the sides of the heavy can. It was past noon; her mother had gone to do the afternoon's cleaning at the Big House, and there was still no sight of Lal on the ridge. Passing the stone barn she eyed the greengages which clung to the wall. They were hard and sour still, but they would be good for pinching in a week or two if the weather kept up. Her mouth was dry. Lifting the can to her lips she drank thirstily and trudged on. When the whistle came she jumped guiltily and brushed the white milky moustache off with her hand. She looked up the ridge. Lal – if indeed it *was* Lal and not Fergie up to something – was a small waving figure at the edge of the birch wood.

Her stomach fluttered. Hurrying up the steps of the house she spilled a few splashes of milk, and had to force herself to set the eggs down carefully on the kitchen table. Then she ran up the ridge, slowing when she came to the wood. Alert for Fergie's nonsense, she slipped through the trees cautiously, making as little noise as an adder, but when she came to the centre of the wood she saw that it was Lal, after all, and a very solid-looking Lal at that. He was lounging comfortably against the Grey Dancer, carving away at the same grey stick with his white knife. He smiled when he saw her creeping towards him, and patted the mossy root beside him.

"Once upon a time, then – aye?"

Annie sat down, keeping her back stiff and

straight against the tree trunk. "Aye," she said, and smiled bravely. "Long ago. . ."

Lal laid down his knife and began: "It was a dark time then," he said slowly, "when they started clearing crofters from the land like you'd sweep flies off a table. But it hadn't yet begun in our county when Isobel came down the mountain, and we didn't much want to hear what she told of the evictions up in Ross. . . ." He paused, and shook his head.

"Anyway, it didn't take Isobel long to set herself up at spinning and dyeing in the village, and she made a living that way. Some of the villagers were not very sure at first – what with Isobel being a spinster woman and living alone, the women were feart for their husbands, withered leg or no withered leg! But by and by, when their bairn took sick or their man turned queer in the head, they'd hear of Isobel's herb medicine, and how the daft grew well when they sat with her while she spun down by the burn, and what words and songs she could soothe the stricken with. And they'd go begging her to come with her bundle to a bad labour, or to sit with a cheery lad who'd taken to greeting and counting dandelion clocks all day, or even to sing at a wake.

"The first summer after she came to Laggan was when I started courting her in earnest. We'd go up on the moor, and then sit here by the tree, and I'd try remembering which herbs were for medicines and which for dyeing, and she'd sit roaring with laughter when I dropped a willowherb into her lap thinking it was a foxglove, or called a hawthorn a rosehip." Lal laughed. "Och, I was ignorant enough then, lass." He picked up his white-handled knife and began to whittle again at the tough grey ash wood. Annie saw that the carving was taking the form of a fish, a fish in the middle of a leap.

"It was aye the carvings she liked. The designs came straight out of my head. Weird and wonderful they were, too, for an untaught crofter lad. Every bird or beast that never lived, as Isobel would say.

"It was here by this tree that I asked her to wed. May, it was, with the smell of clover sweet as never before, and the wild roses in such a bloom as could make your heart burst to see them. And when she said she'd have me, my own heart near did. I didnae know whether to kick my heels in the air or greet like a babe in arms.

"When we went back to Laggan in the twilight, there were those who looked on us kindly – hand in hand we were, with clover sticking in our ears like dafties – but there were aye those who feared such joy, and looked on it dark-faced and superstitious.

"But I wasnae feart of folks' jealousy. I mind I jumped up on the bridge-end and called out to the whole square that the banns would be posted at Crianoch Kirk before the week's end, and that come Midsummer's Eve the drink would flow at our wedding. I raised such a cry that all Laggan came out to stand, and some raised their cups to toast us. But then, in the middle of it all, Isobel pulled at my hand.

'Who cursed us, Lal, did ye no' hear it?' she whispered, her face white as snow.

'No, Isobel, I cannae credit it,' I said, but the cup did a jig in my hand.

'There was one who said, "More than ale will flow at your wedding." Och, Lal, it had a right bitter sound to it.'

"I couldn't sleep that night, thinking of all that had passed, and I went out to smoke a pipe and watch the stars. It was clear and bright, for the moon was well up over Bohespic, and it lit up the carriage that drove through Laggan, so that I could plainly see the jewels of the ladies inside, and the gentrified faces of their menfolk. I glimpsed a gilded coat of arms on the carriage as it rattled past me – and then it was away over the bridge and turning up to Dal. The next morn I slept so long that the cow was fair screaming to be milked; when I woke and went about my work the whisper was all over Laggan that the new owner had come to take Dal estates.

'He's a braw-faced gentleman,' giggled Catriona, who was a kitchen lass at the Big House. 'He gave me a kiss for being so bonny. But his ladies' – she turned her nose up – 'they're sae English I cannae understand the half of their blether.'

'If he gies you kisses you can see tae it that he gies his tenants some improvements,' I said, rightly angrily, for she was always a simpering lass who'd

34

do owt for flattery. 'He'll have to do better than the last laird.'

'He's rich enough, Lal McLennan, to dress his maids in silk gowns and fill the burns wi' claret,' Catriona said pertly. 'The cook says his wealth was made in British India.'

"I thought to myself then that if he'd learned any farming in these parts he couldn't do worse than the old laird, for he'd drunk away his faither's fortune and let the lands of Dal lie fallow. I thought we might all see more oats in the pot, and more beasts in the byre, with the coming of the new one.

"So light-hearted I was, so puffed up with pride about Isobel, that I went dreaming and scheming about the fields that day, seeing here a new iron plough in place of a wood one, and there a barley crop instead of a peat bog. I let on about my thoughts to Isobel and the other tenants, and by the time the sun set that night the whole village was as excited as me. Even old craters who'd known the days of the laird's dungeon were scratching their heads and saying well, they couldnae see the harm in asking. So it was myself and three other young men who were chosen to go to the Big House – tall Gunn and McKinnon's two big gangling sons. We were to greet the new laird, and tell him what wrongs could be righted, what fields could be manured and which drained, where a new forge could be built – och, on and on, a fine plan it was."

Lal jumped to his feet suddenly and pulled Annie up by the hand. "Look down at Laggan, Annie."

He pointed down the valley. "What do you see?"

"Laggan – what else?" Annie squinted against the sun.

"Aye – how big is it?"

"Three cottages, a sweetie shop, and the Laggan bridge. And then there's the new dam further down, the hydroelectric, wi' men working up the sides."

"What else?"

"Sheep."

"Aye. But can you see these hillocks out the back of the Laggan where the ground rises?"

"I see stones and boulders. And an old chimney piece?"

"Ruins. The ruins of cottages. And do you see these ridges that run from the alder grove by the burn to the edge of Bohespic? Fields, there were, between these. Fields of oats and barley and hay. And barns, and cattle too."

Annie looked at Lal. His face was grim and his hand clutched the white knife tightly.

"At first the laird – Cockburn was his name – listened fair and keen to us, and said aye indeed he'd had a taste of farming abroad, in Canada even, and meant to set Dal estates to rights. He told us he had no respect for landlords who managed their estates from the taverns of Edinburgh. He assured us he'd be down to survey the crofts soon enough, and we went away back to our work well pleased with the new man, and brimfull of hopes about changes in the glen."

At the far end of the ridge, by Dal house, Annie glimpsed the laird's green landrover moving silently up the drive between the rhododendron bushes. "It's no' a Cockburn who's laird now, though," she interrupted. "It's Rattray-Douglas."

"Aye. Right enough. The lands of Scotland change hands as often as threepenny bits," Lal said bitterly.

Just then Annie saw her mother coming along the track from Dal to the farm cottages. Lal followed her glance.

"It's your mother?"

"It is." A small white cloud with grey in its belly slipped across the sun, and Annie shivered. "She'll have finished at the Big House."

"She'll be expecting you, then."

"Aye. I've work in the house to do." Annie made no move to go. She fingered the strange half-carved fish that Lal had left lying on a mossy stone.

"I've to go now, too," Lal said hastily. "I've a Co-op delivery to drop at Murchus Lodge." He took the carving gently from her hand. "I'll tell ye the rest another time."

Annie watched him sheath the bone knife in his leather belt. Suddenly she was angry and confused, just like a child next to an adult again.

"Another time," he'd said.

"But why are you telling *me*, anyway," she burst out. "I cannae understand why it's to do with *me*." To Annie her own words seemed to come from far off, like the curlew's plaintive wail.

Lal looked surprised for a moment, and then he began to speak to her in a slow, serious way, as solemn as Westminster Cathedral had been that day, but truer.

"Because , Annie, there are those who beat at you, and bear down on you, and you have it in you to stand firm and brave. And I see in your eyes the wildness – and the longing too, of the old Gaels. Och, I see it often enough in the children, before the Kirks and the Dominies choke it out like life's breath from a wood pigeon." Lal's voice filled with rage, and his hands made a quick twisting in the air, the twist that breaks a neck. "I see you seeking and not finding," he went on, "and Scotland is aye full of those who forget the seeking and live on, never hearing the speak of the land, never noticing their hearts wither within them."

Annie listened quietly to the grand words, not quite believing they were meant for her, and then Lal caught the serious look on her face, and winked at her.

"Dinnae go gettin' a swelled head, though."

Annie shook her head, relieved.

"I'll admit to ye too," he continued, "that a tale like mine grows heavy and bitter wi' no' telling." An oystercatcher wheeled and flew across the valley, and Lal's eyes followed it. "There are times I can hardly bear any more wanderin', and the waitin'."

"What is it you *wait* for?" Annie started to ask, but at that moment her mother appeared by the chicken run outside the cottage. She wore her flowered overall, and carried a pail.

"An-n-n-n-ie," she shouted out, so that her voice echoed thinly across the valley, setting the hens scurrying and rousing the snipe from its secret nest in the heather. She put the pail down and used her hands to shield her eyes from the sun as she looked up at the birch wood. "An-n-n-n-ie," she called again, and beckoned impatiently.

"She's seen us. I'll have to go." Annie started to walk down the hill.

"It's Isobel I wait for." The words came in a whisper behind her, but the wind was stirring such a rustling in the leaves of the Grey Dancer that she couldn't be sure Lal had spoken. She looked back, but saw only a speck in the sky above the wood, wheeling. All the way down the hill her feet went unwillingly, and the words seemed to hang in the bright air around her.

When she reached the cottage yard her mother looked up from feeding the hens and said suspiciously, "Well," she said, "who on earth were ye in that wood wi'?" Her eyebrows shot up in the middle like Kirk steeples.

Annie quailed, "Och, nobody, Mam." She could hear her voice turning into a whine, and she hated it. "It was only Fergie," she lied. "He was setting his rabbit traps."

"Well, just keep away from him, mind," her mother said. "He's a bit simple in the heid."

Annie relaxed. "I ken. I try and avoid him. But

39

he's always sniffin' round his traps."

"Right then. You'll do the dishes, then?" Her mother picked up the pail of corn.

"Aye. But Fergie doesnae scare *me*," Annie added proudly.

*   *   *

On Monday everything went back to normal. Annie and her class filed in to school to find Black Alistair at his high desk by the blackboard. If he was sad about burying his mother, he showed no signs of it. He just sat there, tapping his pointer impatiently on the desk, waiting for them to sit down. Annie thought that there ought to be a way the pupils could all say they were sorry about Mrs Black, but when she got to her desk at the front of the room she looked up at his granite face and saw not a chink of light or warmth there. She shivered, and decided there was no way.

The Headmaster fingered the heavy tawse which lay before him. He rapped once with the pointer and thrust the chalk towards the first row of desks.

"Right. You, Batty. You first. Spelling test. The one I set you to learn last week."

One by one the children went out to the blackboard and tried to write the big words he shouted out, and the others sat nervously waiting their turn. The room was quiet except for the Dominie's voice, the squeak of chalk, and the whistle-slap of the tawse as it came down on the palms of those who got their word wrong. Ian Blain began to sniffle in the back row, and tried to disguise it by blowing his nose; he was worst in the class at spelling.

Annie sat there watching and listening, and eventually she found she was no longer scared, but getting angry instead. When it came to her turn, she crossed her fingers under the desk, held her head high, and stepped out to the board.

"*Embarrassing*," the Dominie called out. "And you'll be embarrassed if you don't get it, all right," he added, so that some of the class tittered.

Annie took a breath, hoped for luck with the 'r's in the middle, and wrote quickly.

Black Alistair looked at the answer and nodded, reluctantly, Annie could have sworn. She walked back to her desk without looking at him, and sat down. There was a silence.

"Just wait a moment, *Miss* Latto." He spoke slowly, in a silky voice. "I've another for you. *Supercilious*. That'll teach you not to come high and mighty with me."

Annie glared at him from under her brows, but there was no sense in protesting, so she got up from her desk and strode to the blackboard. She was standing with the chalk poised to write the first letter when a thought struck her, and the butterflies began to romp in her stomach.

He's asked for it, she thought to herself. It's not fair, what he's doing. She took a breath and concentrated on getting a picture of Lal in her head, for she needed an extra dose of courage for this deed. When she raised the chalk and began to write it was like diving off a high rock into the loch. "TYRANT," she wrote, and came up for air. The blood rushed like a torrent in her veins as she turned to face the Dominie. The class let out a long gasp.

Black Alistair's eyes widened to white for a second, then closed up to slits as he peered at her suspiciously. Annie stood there the picture of innocence. His voice quavered as he said, "*Supercilious*. The word I said was *supercilious*." All the usual sarcasm was gone from his tone.

Annie, sensing that she had won, was able to say quite calmly, "Oh, sorry sir, I must have heard you wrong." Turning back to the board she wrote the word *Supercilious* without a pause. As she put the full stop after it – with a flourish, she couldn't resist that – she heard the class sigh with relief behind her back.

"That'll do for today," the Dominie mumbled, searching under the lid of his desk. "Bring out your English grammars. Quick now!"

The chalk dust danced in a sunbeam from the window as Annie opened her book. With her finger she traced "Thanks, Lal" on the desk.

As soon as the bell went that afternoon Annie hurried towards the bus, wanting to catch Lal for a word before the others piled in. But Sandy McPherson and Ian Blain held her back, asking whether she had cheeked the Dominie on purpose.

"Ye'll no' tell him?" she asked, peering over her shoulder to check that he wasn't in the playground.

The boys shook their heads. "Cross our hearts."

"Aye. I did it on purpose," she said. And she hitched her satchel over her shoulder and strode out of the gate with just the hint of a swagger.

On the bus the two Battys, Mairi McDonald and the Sinclair boys from Murchus had already crammed into the good seats near the driver, and she had to sit behind them, out of earshot of Lal, bursting with the need to tell him. All the way home the Sinclairs rustled their sweetie bags and made Annie prickle with annoyance.

* * *

Crianoch Hall was a corrugated iron building painted dark green, as if to fit in with the pine trees around it. It sat a little way from the village, on the flat ground where Loch Crianoch turned into the shallow rapids of the River Laggan. Ceilidhs and dances were held there, and wedding receptions, and Sales of Work put on by the Women's Institute. Annie had played many a wild and scary game of hide-and-seek there, outside in the dark fragrant wood, while inside the adults careered round the floor in the Gay Gordons or Strip the Willow.

This time, though, there was no entertainment planned, since it was only a meeting about the dam, and few people bothered to attend those. Annie went along with her dad for the drive – and maybe too, she thought, as the Baby Austin turned over Crianoch Bridge, maybe she'd run into Lal.

A man with a posh accent was already speaking from the stage when Annie and her dad went into the hall. He was waving a pointer back and forth across a big white map. "And here we have the hills of Murchus," he was saying to the half-empty benches. He stuttered over the Scottish word. "And now here, due east. . . ." – the pointer moved across the white plastic with a squeak – "here you see the estates of Dal marked in blue. . . and further east, in the valley, the hamlet of Laggan." His deerstalker and his accent made Annie want to giggle, and she nudged her dad to share it with him; but his face was stern, his eyes cold with anger. He was staring at the men on the stage, concentrating hard.

"Now this should be no matter for con*trov*ersy," the gent drawled; Annie wondered if that was the proper English pronunciation. "After all, the compensation had been accepted by Mr Sinclair. . ." – he nodded towards the ruddy-cheeked Sinclair, who sat beaming in the front row – ". . . and Mr Rattray-Douglas whose famous Dal grouse moors are no longer threatened."

44

Annie shifted restlessly on the creaky bench. "Dad," she whispered, "I'm going out to the toilet."

"On ye go, then," he whispered back, with one eye still fixed on the speaker. Annie tiptoed out of the hall and raced off through the fine-smelling pines to the stony river bank. Straight across the river she could see the back of the Co-op garage, and beyond it, built on to the Co-op stores, Lal's house with its creosoted wood walls and silvery tin roof. The river was shallow at the rapids, and it was shorter to cross there than to go all the way round by the bridge, so she tucked her dress into her knickers and with her sandals in her hand, waded through the rushing cold water. When she reached the other side, her feet were freezing and scarlet from it, and the grassy bank was warm under her bare toes.

She found Lal in the garage yard cleaning the spark plugs from the bus. When he squeezed her hand to say hello he left oily marks on her skin.

"I've the kettle on the boil upstairs. Will ye take tea in my parlour, Miss?" he joked.

The white room was as cool and dreamy as before, with a jug of buttercups glowing yellow on the mantelpiece. Annie hung around Lal in the kitchen, saying, "Let me do it. I'll help," but he shooshed her out and made her sit in the rocker. Pushing against the carpet with toes that were still mottled from the river, she rocked herself and shouted the tale of Black Alistair and the spelling test through the open door to him, hardly boasting at all.

"Good lass," Lal said, sticking his face round the door. "That'll teach him."

After the tea was made and laid alongside a packet of Rich Tea biscuits on the shiny red table, Annie stopped rocking. She cleared her throat. "Tell me more of Isobel now," she said, hoping it didn't sound too cheeky. "Did you really say you were *waiting* for her?" Her voice trembled.

Lal sighed, and set down his tea. From a drawer in the table he took the half-finished carving, and sat holding it awhile, stroking it with his thumbs. He stared and stared at it, until Annie thought he had forgotten her presence altogether. After what seemed like a long time she heard him say very softly, in a singsong voice, "By Laggan burn, I'll wait, until the turning. Each Midsummer's Eve, at twilight, when the fish are rising."

To Annie it sounded more like a song than anything, like an old lament he was singing to himself. Its quiet spell lulled her, and she sat waiting in a great stillness, the stillness she had sometimes felt as a babe at her grandmother's knee.

He reached for the white knife and the spell was broken. Whittling, he carried on with his story, quite naturally, as if he had never stopped.

"We heard that the laird had his fingers in sheep-farming, but we didnae think too hard about a few sheep on the moors – as busy folk dinnae think about what's not under their noses yet. So we went about our business, and bided our time till the laird and his factor saw fit to come around the Laggan crofts.

"Isobel was busy at her spinning, and what wi' that and tending at sickbeds and making her wedding clothes, she scarce had time to take a walk on the moor or gather a bunch of wild flowers for her table. The next Sunday, though, she came to Crianoch wi' me, to post the banns at the Kirk. I set her on McKinnon's old piebald horse which he'd lent for the day, and walked beside her all the road to Crianoch. And when we came down Crianoch brae, my head was so high in the air, you'd have thought I had the Queen of the Fairies herself for company.

"It was chill and damp in the Kirk, though, and the wee clerk had a mouth like a seam and a big pimple on his nose, and he looked at Isobel right queer when he wrote down the names. He went like the clappers to get through the paperwork, and got it over with at such a rate that Isobel banged my knee under the table and whispered that he must think we were going to gie him the Evil Eye. I had to put my hand o'er my face to stop frae laughing.

"Such were our high spirits that it took us a long time wandering back to Laggan. First Isobel got me to gather hawthorn and bride's blossom and wild yellow iris to weave around the old nag's neck. Then we had to stop to paddle in this or that burn or to pick blaeberries till our hands and mouths were the colour of the old Picts. So – the sun was low and the bracken on the hills was fierce russet with it when we came in sight of Laggan Bridge.

"McKinnon hailed me before we entered the village, and rolled his eyes at the sight of his horse, all wreathed with flowers and berries. 'The factor's been,' he said, 'it doesnae sound good. He's been a' round the crofts wi' his books and accountin'. Cockburn's skulkin' up Dal sayin' the estate's near bankrupt and the Cheviot herds are doin' well for his cousins up at Badenoch.'

"'Badenoch,' Isobel hissed. 'Ye ken what passed there!' Her eyes flashed with anger. 'The lairds fining folk whose cattle strayed on their sheepwalks. Four hundred souls put out frae their homes, to wander the coasts at the herring fishing. And half of them shipped away tae Canada!'

"'Aye,' I said, soothing-like, 'but Cockburn doesnae seem like one of they rascals tae me. And I've aye said there's room for both folks and sheep on these acres. He'll see reason,' I said, firm as anything, though I didn't feel it.

"McKinnon glowered at me. 'No, Lal,' he said, gripping my arm in his big blacksmith's hand. 'Murdoch's son Hamish sent word that his regiment's aye at the ready at Fort George. To be sent against their ane people, Lal. Och, there's terrible tales now. Folk say that the glens of Ross are near empty in this last year.'

"'Aye, there's action to be taken, and fast,' Isobel said, with a face like flint, which to my mind went ill with her mount, which was still as gay as a May

Fair. I'll admit I wasnae used to such words from a lass, and I thought it didnae become women to take a lead. Oh, in the end I could see the sense in what Isobel and McKinnon said, but it was still a sulky Lal McLellan who stopped Catriona on her way to work the next morn and gave her a message for Cockburn. The gist of the message was that myself, Murdoch, Gunn and McKinnon would attend at Dal that afternoon to get some honest talk out of the laird.

"At first Catriona refused to do the errand for us. 'Makin' trouble again, Lal McLennan,' she said, with an uppity look.

"'It's your maister who seeks trouble, no' me,' I snapped, hoping to put some sense into her silly heid. But she just stuck out her tongue at me, and prinked up the new black ribbon in her hair.

"Then she came near and whispered in my ear, 'I'll take your message, but only if ye'll gie me a dance and a kiss at your wedding.'

"'Awa' wi' ye,' I said, fair fed up with her. 'That Big House is making ye into a right wanton.' I turned on my heel, saying, 'Just you mind that message gets to the laird, or it'll be the worse for you.'

"'At least I've *two* good legs for dancing,' she spat after me. 'No' like some lasses I could mention,' and before I could catch her and gie her the clout she deserved she was away scurrying across the bridge with her skirts flapping.

"In any case, the message must have got to

Cockburn, for when we attended at Dal the laird was sat ready in his velvet chair, with his snuffbox at his elbow and a wee spaniel licking round his ankles.

"'Of course, the glen was already going to rack and ruin before. Mr Farquharson, the last laird, died,' Cockburn said, and his wee pink nose twitched like a rabbit. 'In fact, the use of the land was, and is, uneconomic.' On and on he talked, to his dog or to the chandelier, it seemed, for he never looked us in the eye.

"He paused every now and then to take a pinch of snuff very daintily, or to look over at his skinny-legged factor, who stood nodding at everything he said. But by and by he came to the meat of the matter.

"'I'm very interested in your plans for improvement,' he drawled, 'and I'm willing to go along with them – or some of them – as long as they fit in with my plans for a Cheviot herd.' Cockburn nodded his head towards the factor.

"'But Mr Innes will explain better than I can.'

"Innes the factor stood ill at ease on the big rich rug in front of the fireplace. He unrolled a bit of paper and reeled off the number of tenants, subtenants and cotters on Dal estate."

Lal took a deep breath. "You see, Annie, Cockburn was offering us a deal, and dirty work it was. He wanted thirty-five folks off his land, and the rest of us were promised the benefits of the sheep and the improvements we'd talked of. When the factor came out with all this McKinnon went purple in the face wi' fury, and stepped forward. 'Beggin' your pardon, Mister Cockburn,' he said, right sarcastic, 'but the thirty-five folks sent off to wander the county will only be the first, am I right? Oh aye, I've heard tell of how your sort proceed. First three tenants and their subtenants, and then another three, and so on till there's not a soul tae be seen across the glen. Just the four-legged ones wi' woolly coats.'

"Cockburn rose from his chair. 'I'm sorry that you gentlemen see it that way. Nevertheless, my factor will be issuing the writs of removal forthwith. Good day to you.' And with that he tucked the spaniel under his arm and made for the door.

"'Oh, no, Mr Cockburn. It's no' good-day yet,' I cried, stepping out at him, and getting a grip on his collar, I was that wild. Cockburn took fright and dropped the whining dog. 'There'll be no notices of eviction served on Laggan folk who've farmed these lands for centuries afore your kind set foot here. Try bringing your notices and they'll burn in your hands.' I had hold of him by the neckcloth and was going to shake him like a rat, but Murdoch and Gunn pulled me back.

"'Rash words, McLennan,' Cockburn squeaked, from behind the factor, who was white round the gills himself. 'Mind you don't regret them. I have the due process of the Law behind me, you understand.'

"That night there was a hush over Laggan, as if

folks were trying to take in the terrible news. The next morn, we made our plans. In case the sherriff and his constables came, the older bairns were to sit up by the peat-cuttings and watch the comings and goings at Dal. Each day they were to keep watch on the road. Groups of lads raided Dal woods for tough ash sticks, and trimmed and stowed them away under the straw in the byres. Even old muskets were cleaned and made ready – though there were some of us who never thought it would come to shots. Young lasses gathered good-sized throwing stones on the river bank and set them in piles by the bridge at one end of Laggan and by the smithy at the other.

"Isobel herself was everywhere, to tell the truth you'd have thought she was a general in the Argyll and Sutherland Highlanders. She hurried around, a real sight with her hair scraped back in a red shawl and greasy marks on her face, showing the lasses how to bind hemp torches. Or else – and we laughed at her for this – she was busy into the night sewing stiff corsets to protect the women from cudgel blows. For Isobel, under her gentle looks, was a fierce one, one of those who believed it would go that far, and farther.

"From morn till night we worked in the fields wi' one eye on the road and our ears cocked for a whistle from the bairns which would warn us the constables were marching on us. But day followed day and neither lawmakers nor laird's men were seen.

"What was sighted, though, by the lookouts at the peat-stacks, was a wee clerk on a skinny black horse which could hardly totter over the humped bridge into Laggan. Before this apparition got to the bridge end, Isobel was there, waiting with her hands on her hips and the other lasses coming up behind.

"I saw her take the paper from his hand and look at it, and then she came limping fast up the rig towards me. I dropped my hoe and ran for her.

"'It's the Kirk Session,' she panted, with her scarf askew and her hair falling in her eyes. 'They've called *me* to the Kirk Session. And they willnae put up the banns, Lal.' She sank down in the heather. 'They willnae wed us, Lal, I should have known it.'

"I took the paper from her hand. It was a summons for her to attend that week's Sessions in Crianoch, where they meant to put her on trial for "Unlawful practices and Irreligious conduct." It was a witch hunt, as plain as day. A witch hunt such as we hadnae seen for many a year.

"'Come on, Isobel, ye're no feart of these old bible thumpers,' I said, to cheer her. 'They can do nowt. They can rant and try to shame you in front of the village – but they've neither the grounds nor the power to convict ye of owt.'

"She bore up then, and stayed strong-hearted until two days after, when we made the journey to Crianoch. We were right pleased to have brought well-wishers with us when we saw what was ranged against us in the Kirk Hall. For my lord Cockburn sat there po-faced on his fine cushioned pew, and Innes the factor, and the minister, and all the Auld Kirk elders. And lo and behold, Catriona was there among Cockburn's retinue, sitting shifty-eyed and white as a shroud.

"But as for us, we had sturdy McFie and his two wild daughters, and Margaret Murdoch, and the big laughing Gunn, and McKinnon's lads.

"'Our lord Cockburn's no' here tae see God's work done,' Margaret Murdoch whispered to Isobel. 'Mair like the devil's.'

"'He's out tae turn folks against ye because you spoke out,' Gunn said in my ear.

"Isobel was led by the pimple-faced clerk up to the stool, where she had to stand while the minister read out the accusations against her. And then our own Catriona was called to be questioned. I felt sorry for Catriona at first, looking at the wild, scared state of her, and the way her hands kept plucking at her bodice strings. But when I heard her answers – you had to strain to hear her – I was no longer sorry. I felt she was no longer kin of mine and had no place in Laggan from that day on. The lies came slithering off her lips like watersnakes into a pond, shrivelling the hearts of us who listened.

"She said, 'Yes, sir, the woman telt me how to get rid of the bairn wi' herbs and potions, and said a spell over my belly. But I didnae take the potions, sir. I want the bairn, even though it'll have no faither.'

"'And the father of the child?' said the minister.

"'Lachlan McLennan, sir,' she mumbled, stealing a glance across at Cockburn. There was a gasp from our folk, and all eyes fixed on Catriona, in amazement at the treachery of it. Catriona was led back to her seat to the sound of hissing from the Laggan folk, and she sat there with her head well down.

"Isobel was left alone in the middle of the room then. The sun squeezed in through the mean wee window arch and settled on her hair; she drew herself up in that tight wee byre of a place so that she looked as tall as an ancient warrior woman, and her hair was like a flame licking at the roof beams.

"The elders gaped, the minster dropped his felt hat, and all were silenced. Myself, I even had the fear of fairies within me, watching her there.

"'It is a healer I am,' she said, her voice ringing out. 'And it's the few skills I've learned I give to all who ask. As for the girl Catriona. . .' – Isobel looked scornfully at her – 'she never asked help of me. Except in the way of lovecharms I couldnae give her, for I'm no magician to make a man love where he doesnae.' She turned to the minister, the laird, and the elders with a look of contempt. 'As for you crows and bigots, laird's creatures, your marriage blessings would set a blight on lads and girls alike. You'd freeze passion like a frog under ice and then poke at it and call it sin and ugliness.' Her eyes narrowed and raked the benches accusingly. 'And then, everybody kens, there's one among you comes

55

creeping to spy on the lasses bathing in the burn.' The elders seemed to shrink inside their black cloth and from the benches where the ordinary folk sat came a ripple of laughter.

"'It's true,' Fiona McFie shouted boldly.

"'Aye,' Isobel went on. 'We can tell a felt hat from an alder bush all right.' She waited till the snorts of laughter and cries of 'for shame' had died down. Then she pointed straight across to me.

"'This is my man,' she said, 'and I'll have him.' My knees knocked and I blushed like fire, I was that taken aback, and shamefully, I was so feart I near foreswore her there and then. Murdoch put his arm in mine, and bore me up as she continued.

"'And I'll make my wedding,' she went on, in an ancient lilting voice that was Isobel's and yet was not. 'Aye, I'll make it under high heaven, on the moor where there's beasts that stand straight and dinnae crawl, where there's fine air to breathe instead o' the reek of mealy-mouthed lies. Be damned to you!' And she stepped down off the stool so that the sunbeam, losing her hair, seemed to go out of the place.

"I ran and took her arm, and the others banded round us in a ring, and in that way we hurried out of the square and away on the horses back to Laggan. All the way back we shouted to each other over the noise of the wind and the clatter of hooves, that if the minister didn't move against Laggan, the laird would. We must keep eyes and ears skinned, and make Laggan ready against the bleak times that were on us.

"That night Isobel woke in the small hours and came rapping at my door. She wept as she told me how she had dreamed of all the people banished from the glen, the house timbers blackened and burned, the crops choked with bracken, and the land left to the sheep herds and the curlews. I comforted her as best I could, taking her on my knee and stroking her tangled hair away from her brow. 'Hush, Isobel, hush now. You said yourself we must fight,' I reminded her. 'If Cockburn will shift us from our glen, he must battle us for it.' I tied a shawl round her, and after a while her shaking eased and her teeth stopped chattering. But her eyes still looked queer and faraway, as if peering into the depths of a pool which others couldn't fathom.

"'Soon,' she said suddenly, 'soon they'll come after us.' I rocked and hushed her some more, until her cheeks got some of their rosy colour back, and her head began to nod sleepily against my shoulder. 'Tomorrow is Midsummer's Eve, Lal,' she murmured, cuddling up.

"'It is indeed.' In all the trouble, I'd near forgotten.

"'We'll wed, then, as we planned? There's no sense in waiting now.'

"'Aye, we will that,' I replied, and squeezed her till she said to mind and leave her some ribs for her wedding day.

"At noon the next day I threw down hoe and spade and went to make ready. I had a new white shirt sewed by Margaret Murdoch, and Isobel herself had spun the cloth for my breeches. Before long I was clean and spruce and striding up the ridge, skirting Dal, to the birch wood hill. I had time for a pipe to calm myself down before Isobel came, alone, across the burn at the bottom of the hill. She wore a plain green gown, and carried in her hand a bunch of wild rye grasses. As she climbed the hill through the trees she called out, 'Today we must play both minister and betrothed, then, Lal.'

"'*You* must,' I said, 'for I haven't the words.'

"And so she did, in her own fashion, in the way she said she'd learnt from her grandmother over the mountains. She took the lower branches of the big tree, the one you call the Grey Dancer, and twisted them together to form a wreath. And then she called me to come inside and kiss in the wreath. Then with a laugh she stripped the pale ears from the rye grass and scattered them over us both, as if they were oats from the harvest.

"Then she did something that made my blood turn watery in my veins, with the old superstition. She called out to Bride, goddess of the old religion of which I'd heard tell.

"'Mother of fire and of crops,' she cried, with her head thrown back and her arms raised up. 'Witness now that we are wedded and pledged in this glen and by this glen, and will bide on among the fields and rocks and burns of this glen, witness us that.' I stood shivering in the midsummer's heat, listening to her.

"'Enough, lass, let's away now,' I urged, but she paid no heed. And then she went on to chant the lines of some ancient blessing, of wedding or of harvest, she told me.

'The mother of birch trees keens a high song.
The mother of landslides is heavy-hipped.
The mother of rainbows speaks glory.'

"Afterwards she smiled and untied the wreath from about us, so that the branches sprang back into place with their leaves shaking and whispering. And in that way we were wed, without priest or prayer book, on the open heath.

"That night our wedding supper was laid out in Isobel's cottage by the burn. There was ale and whisky, meat and game, and oatcakes, cheese, and all manner of currant jams. There were those in Laggan who stayed away, seeing as it was no proper church wedding, but most came, at least to drink our health.

"McKinnon fiddled, and Flora sang, and there was dancing too, for those who wanted. Catriona, though – Catriona of the lying tongue who had wanted sore to dance at my wedding – was nowhere to be seen, nor was she missed. Folks said she had carried away her belongings to Dal house, and was to bide there and have her bairn – if indeed there was a bairn at all.

"Despite the threat that hung over Laggan, our neighbours did fine at putting away their worries that night, and it was a glad enough time we had. It was well past midnight when the music died down and the last company staggered away home, and Isobel and I went to sleep that night as content as any bride and groom in the land.

"It was from the depths of sweet dreams that a bellowing of beasts in the yard woke us. With my eyes stuck tight with sleep I made to jump out of bed and see to the cows – I though a wildcat was at them – but then the smoke hit my lungs with a searing pain. Racked with coughs, I tried to rouse Isobel, but she lay there senseless, and her face was grey as ashes in the flickering light. The roof was on fire, and the thatch was beginning to fall in big flaming swathes. Burning straw and showers of sparks were setting the furniture alight. I started to shout for help and began dragging Isobel's limp form towards the door, swatting like a madman at the sparks which set flames licking at her nightgown.

"From outside I heard a faint shout over the noise of the flames. 'Get the door open, man! Lal, Lal, the door's jammed!'

"I left Isobel for a moment to grope my way through the reek of smoke to the water pail, and dragged wet cloths back to throw over us. Above me I heard the roof timbers creak. Through my streaming eyes I saw how the beam above the door had sagged and jammed it. One had near burnt through, and I knew then that we had no time at all. I had to get Isobel to the window. But in between was the bed burning, and the flaming sheaves falling – a scarlet sheet of fire like a sight of hell's furnaces.

"Just then Isobel stirred. Her big eyes looked up at me out of her smoke-grimed face. Her hair was all singed and burnt, and sleeked with wet from the towel, and her poor legs were scarred and blackened under the rags of her shift. She opened her mouth to speak but could not move her parched lips.

"'Be brave, Isobel,' I said, 'for we must go through the fire.' But she looked at me with no sign of understanding. I swathed the wet cloths about our heads then, and lifting Isobel up, I took my belt and lashed her to my breast like a babe to its mother. Then with half a prayer to any god who might be listening, I plunged into the fire.

"I remember little then but the agony all over and around me, and inside me, as the fiery air scourged my lungs, and then a roar of whiteness. And then nothing. For an age, nothing.

"The water brought consciousness back to me, not that I wanted it then, nor for a long time after. I was lying in the stony shallows of the burn; Murdoch and Gunn were leaning over me.

"'We had to dowse the flames off you, Lal,' Gunn said. Tears were dribbling down his big freckled face, a rare enough sight, I thought dimly to myself, and I smiled up at him like a daftie.

"'Forgive us, Lal, forgive us,' Murdoch was muttering, 'We missed the watch.' Gunn elbowed him and said, 'Wheesht, man, for God's sake.'

"Then I heard Margaret's voice crooning soft nearby. 'There, lass, there now, dinnae move, lass,' it went, and I knew who it was meant for.

"I caught hold of Gunn's coat with a hand that I didn't know for a minute, such a black claw-like thing it was. 'Get me near her. Get me to Isobel.'

"They lifted me then, the two of them, and I saw the night sky above me not black, but red with fire and with pain. They set me down at the water's edge where Isobel lay among the reeds with Margaret's arm around her.

"She saw me then, and made a sign at me to come closer. Her dry lips were trying to form words. I put my ear to her face, and could barely hear the faint croak of her voice.

"'Lal,' she whispered, 'mind that Bride is the mother of fire. Of the fire that transforms,' She tried to touch my cheek with her cracked lips. 'And we will bide on here. Mind that, Lal.' She sighed then, and her head dropped back, and her eyes stared at the stars.

"Margaret held me and said gently, 'She's gone, Lal, she's gone. Lord rest her soul.'

"'Not gone,' I howled out then. 'Not gone.' And then such a roaring started in my breast, a screeching and crackling as if the fire was on me once more; the light around me grew and grew, burning blue-white until it shone through the grass to the earth beneath, and to the granite beneath that; and when I looked at my own burned skin, I saw only the white bones underneath, like the black bark of hawthorn peels to the white pith.

"I looked at Isobel and saw her bones clear and frail in the radiance. And then there was the turning. I saw it in Isobel as a floating, a drifting of particles. Under my eyes her white bones were suddenly like a cloud of moths which, startled, flew up, and fluttered, and hung, and came to rest again in a changed pattern.

"In myself I felt it first like a blind white pain, a tearing, and then a lightness and a freedom. A hiss of wind was in my ears, and I was soaring, while down in the burn Isobel was slipping ever deeper in the water, with her new long shape and her silver scales gleaming up at me. . ."

On the mantelpiece the clock chimed with a sudden clang, and Annie gasped with fright. Lal looked up from his whittling.

"I know, lass, it's an awful tale. But don't be feart. It's all gone and done wi' now." He held up the finished carving to the light; it had taken the form of a trout, leaping and twisting.

Annie realized that her face was soaked with tears. "It was a trout, then, she became."

"Aye, and I was turned to the golden eagle, to fly and perch among these mountains until such time as another change will come."

"But is she still in the burn, as well?" Annie's heart nearly stopped, remembering the times she'd fished there with her father. It didn't bear thinking about. She saw the clean leap and splash of trout rising on a summer evening. She saw the menacing way the worm on the line trailed down to the bottom of the burn, and wriggled and bounced across the stones and through the eddies as her dad walked downstream with the rod. She saw the panic-stricken writhing of the fish as the hook caught and the line dragged.

"Oh, Lal, is she there yet?" she cried out.

"Aye, Annie, she is, sure enough," Lal calmed her. "Every year, near Midsummer, I come here to the glen, and I wait and I watch for her. In sun or storm, I watch by the fork in the burn, near the reeds, and always she comes."

"Laggan burn?" A thought struck Annie. "But are they no' flooding there, the hydroelectric?" she said, remembering the meeting. "I'll have to get back, too. My dad's down at the Hall listening to them."

"I'll walk ye'."

"The burn will go, won't it?" Annie asked as they walked towards the river.

"It will." Lal sighed. "Maybe it's as well."

Annie was shocked. "What's as well?"

"For the place to be gone. No' to go on waiting for the turning, hoping all these years for it."

"But this Midsummer, ye'll wait?"

"Surely."

They walked in silence for a while, looking at the hot colours the sunset spread over the slate roofs of Crianoch. Fish snapped at flies on the surface of the loch, making circular ripples. Annie's thoughts strayed back to Laggan.

"Were the other cottages fired too?" she asked.

"No, not that night. But later, for the villagers still resisted Cockburn, even after he'd got the ringleaders, as he called us. The sheriff and his constables came with the writs, and a regiment was even standing by – but they still fought them, the women fiercest. Young Flora McKinnon and Margaret Murdoch were taken away to Inverness gaol, and mouldered there for a year. And one by one the cotters were put out, and the house timbers pulled down and burnt, until Laggan was as fine and empty as the laird wanted, for his sheepwalk."

"And that was the end?" Annie was numb at the thought of all the injustice that had passed in her glen.

"Aye. That was the finish of the settlement at Laggan." Lal reached over and grasped Annie's hand. "Never forget that tale, Annie," he said urgently. "Whatever happens, wherever ye' go, remember what happened here and in other glens of Scotland. So when your teachers stuff you with pap about the braw Queen and her Commonwealth and the great Empire, mind some of the crimes that were done in the building of it."

Together they waded the shallows of the river, and came up the grassy bank to the Hall. They went round to the back door, where no one would notice them. The meeting was still going on.

* * *

The tweedy gentleman rolled up his map. "To sum up," he announced, "the six occupants of Laggan have accepted the Board's compensation, as has Mr Rattray-Douglas, for the small portion of his land which will be affected." Annie nudged Lal and he nodded grimly. The man on the stage went on. "In a week's time we'll be running water down the new Bohespic tunnel from Loch Quoyle, and starting up the turbines. The water levels in Laggan valley will only begin to rise very gradually towards the end of the month."

Annie saw her dad's hand go up in the second row, and she caught her breath. But the speaker waved him down. "Please, Mr Latto, your remarks will be passed to the relevant department, I assure you."

The meeting finished with a scraping of chairs and an explosion of every cough and splutter the audience had been containing during the speeches. Annie and Lal met her father outside.

"There ye' are," he said, lighting up a Players and taking a good drag on it. "Och, what a damned farce that was!" He saw Lal and nodded. "Garage all right?"

"Fine, Mr Latto."

"You're liking the job, then?"

"I like it fine," Lal smiled shyly.

"Even wi' old sourpuss for the boss?"

"Thomson? Oh Aye." Lal laughed out loud.

"He is and all." Lal gestured vaguely at Annie. "I met your daughter out walking."

"Nosing around the garage, was she?" her father said indulgently. "She's a tearaway."

"A fine lass you've got," said Lal, and Annie glowed, feeling shy and strange between the two of them.

She stared at her feet in embarrassment. Her toes caught a daisy in the grass, and twisted it, so that it broke from its stem.

"Can I just ask, Mr Latto," said Lal, "what was it you said about Bohespic tunnel to put the wind up the speaker?"

Annie saw her father's face darken with anger. "I said the truth, like I've been sayin' all along. But they willnae hear it," he said bitterly, "they're in such a damned rush to turn this glen into a fishpond." He drew on his cigarette. "From what I've seen at the works, I cannae be certain the tunnel construction's safe. There's been accidents, too. Hushed up, ye understand. The building contractors – they cut corners, ye ken." He blew the cigarette smoke out in a long blue plume. "Nobody talks about the leaks and cave-ins – just the men who get injured in them." He put his hand on Annie's shoulder and walked slowly towards the car. As he started the engine he said to Lal, "The whole of Loch Quoyle could pile down that tunnel into the glen, if owt went wrong." He sounded very tired, and coughed raspingly. "That's what they're playing wi'."

As the car drew away, Annie looked back. Lal stood staring after it, brooding.

Annie turned to her dad. "But our school picnic's up Loch Quoyle this year. The Head said we could see the new dam start up from the hill. Won't it be safe, then?" she asked anxiously.

Her dad glanced quickly at her. "Och, don't worry your head, lass. You're safe enough up the top of Bohespic." He paused to put his cigarette out. "It's down below that's the worry."

* * *

For the picnic, Annie had asked for sardine and egg sandwiches, but she got ham paste instead.

"Well, you can share around, can't ye?" her mother said when Annie opened her mouth to grumble, and rushed off to work.

Black Alistair had insisted that they all assemble at the school first, so it was odd to get the bus all the way to Crianoch and then file back in again and drive all the way back past Dal and past the fork where the burn met the Laggan river – Isobel's fork, as Annie called it now. They parked a mile downstream from the dam, where the Laggan was a near-dry bed of limy white stones and cracked grey mud. At the roadside where the bus stopped, tinkers had made their camp, and the marks of their stay were still visible. Birch saplings had been left bent over and lashed to the ground, the framework for their tarpaulin tents. A circle of blackened stones containing ash and tin cans was all that remained of their cooking fire.

Black Alistair turned up his nose at the place and led them past with a flourish of his walking stick. He walked differently in his thick hiking boots, and his school flannels were tucked into long hairy socks.

A narrow track led from the camp up the shoulder of Bohespic. It wound through a chestnut grove, and then turned steeply up through a wood of larch, and a grove of dwarf oaks with their blue beards of lichen.

In a clearing in the larch wood, Annie stopped to look down on the curved face of the dam. It looked magnificent and strange, like a big white shell blocking the end of the valley. From where she was, the workers looked quite tiny, like crawling wasps in their yellow hats. She stood for a while, slightly dizzy from the climb, and wondered about what her dad had said. Everything looked thick and safe and solid to her, but then she hadn't seen the tunnel yet.

She began to climb again, and caught a glimpse of a reddish scar in the hillside which she had seen before from a long way off. It was a deep channel, crisscrossed by bulldozer tracks. Snaking down the middle of the cleft all the way to the dam were two huge pipes, jointed and riveted and painted bright orange. Up ahead, a light chattering of voices was the rest of the school.

Suddenly a footstep behind her broke the daydream.

"Get a move on, Annie Latto," Black Alistair's voice said, booming out in the quiet wood. "You haven't got all day."

Annie realized that he must have circled back without her noticing, and she started to hurry up the hill while his hiking boots trod the bracken close behind her.

Above the dwarf oaks the path grew steeper, and ran straight up beside the big pipes. Soon Annie was hot and sweating, for there was neither wind nor shade on the open slope. Her socks were creeping down and round her heels, rucking up uncomfortably under her feet. She stopped to take her sandals off and pull the socks straight, but Black Alistair stopped behind her.

"Don't dawdle, Annie," he said, standing over her. "I don't like dawdlers. Even clever ones." He smiled slyly, and moved away a few paces. Annie saw him break a branch from a young birch tree by the path. When she began to climb again, she could hear him behind her stripping the leaves off. Then, to her horror, she suddenly felt a stinging pain across the back of her legs. He had lashed her with it. She looked round at him, still unable to believe he'd done it deliberately. He smiled at her, a frightening, playful sort of smile, and gave her legs another taste of it.

She leapt back. "I cannae go faster," she protested.

"No? Well, we'll see about that."

And then Annie did move. Fear made her short legs pound up the slope, as she tried desperately to catch up with the others. But they were well ahead, up by the steel doors at the entrance to the tunnel. Black Alistair easily kept up with her, and the lash of the birch whip came more often. Annie's breath came in gasps as she fought her way up the slope, and tears were beginning to blind her. If she could just keep going, just a bit farther, she might see her dad or one of his mates working up at the tunnel.

"What's he doing this *for*?" she thought, confusedly, and then the fiery pain in her lungs stopped her, and she collapsed on the path, panting harsh breaths. And Black Alistair was above her, with the birch branch raised, and that terrible teasing smile on his face.

It was then that she felt a kind of hissing in the air, a stirring in the bracken that was like a sigh. And she remembered. With all the strength that was in her suddenly set free, she jumped to her feet. Her eyes blazed as she snatched the whip from the Headmaster's hand, and slashed him once, hard, across the cheek.

"Don't ever," she hissed, "don't *ever* do that to me!"

Black Alistair put one hand up to his face. He stared at her in shock, while the blood started to run. "You've cut me," he said stupidly.

"You asked for it, you old brute," she snapped, and made to race off, beginning to feel dread now at what she had done. But Black Alistair recovered himself quickly, and came hammering behind her, shouting, "You're for it now, you wee witch."

His hand caught the back of her dress, and she felt herself lifted by the scruff of the neck and swung through the air. The sun danced a mad reel in the sky above her.

And then there was an extra glimmer of gold up there. Annie gasped, for as Lal plummeted from the skies he was a terrible sight. An eagle the size of a man, with an eye of fire, a queer long body and wings ten feet across. Black Alistair fell back in horror when he saw the bird diving for him, but Lal only brushed him with a wing tip, and came to rest on a rocky shelf above him.

Alistair stared up, hypnotized.

Then came the turning: all shimmer and light and a buzzing behind Annie's eyes. She closed them for a moment to shut out the glare, and saw Lal there on the rock in his human form, pointing one arm straight and fierce at the Headmaster. But when she opened them again there was only the huge bird with its wings outstretched above her. And then, as if inside her head, Lal's voice began to beat like a drum.

"One more finger laid on Annie," the voice said, "one finger laid on any child of the glen, and I'll fly that miserable flesh over the mountain and drop it to the bottom of Loch Ericht for the pike to nibble on."

And then the eagle's wings beat hard, and its great weight hung in the air above Black Alistair's head, with its claws flashing within an inch of his eyes.

Alistair fell to his knees and whimpered then. Annie saw him cower down as meek and scared as any bairn he'd ever walloped, and her heart was light.

Inside her head the voice sounded again. "You can be proud of this day's work, lass." And the eagle was gone in a ripple of air, swooping across the valley.

Annie took one look at Black Alistair's dust-streaked face with the red weal across it. Then she turned her back and marched on up the hill.

* * *

All day, the Headmaster was silent and ashen-faced. It was left to a confused Miss Boyd to point out this or that thing about the tunnel and its workings, and to give the school Nature Study at Loch Quoyle.

Loch Quoyle sheltered in a big saucer in Bohespic Hill like lava in the top of a volcano. From the brim of the saucer, you could look straight down on the dam and, beside it, the blockhouses of the generating station. So it was there they all assembled, joking and chattering and eating their crisps and apples left over from lunch, to watch the midget figures swarm far below. Annie sat chewing a hazel twig and waiting for the dam to start working.

At three o'clock sharp there was a faint rumble under the hill – or so Alec Batty, with his ear to the heather and his backside in midair – insisted. Then down below a turbulence began in the water behind the dam, a sucking and swirling. Soon after, the water began to spurt out, white and frothed by the unseen propellers. A cheer went up from the children, and Sandy McFie made a one-gun salute with his empty crisp bag and sent Annie a foot into the air with fright. She scowled at Sandy and went on watching, with her nerves strung tight, for something to go wrong. For a big crack to zigzag across the dam, or the steel doors of the tunnel to bulge and gape open under the weight of all the water in Loch Quoyle. Along the hill Black Alistair sat, alone and still as a rock, as if he was waiting too, waiting in the eerieness for a crack or a splinter.

But nothing happened. The midge-sized figures moved unharmed about the surface of the dam, and the steel stairs and platforms stayed safe and strong while the white waters foamed neatly enough down two of the six outflow channels.

Nevertheless it was not a sure Annie who picked her way pigeon-toed down the slope to the road. Her knees felt wobbly and she kept well clear of the Headmaster. Luckily he left the path before the tinker camp, muttering something about taking a look over the dam, and leaving Miss Boyd to see the pupils home.

In the bus Annie captured the seat behind Lal. Under cover of the noise and the shoving as the others jostled for their seats she whispered, "You fixed Black Alistair all right. There's no' been a peep out of him all day."

"The two of us, Annie," he reminded. "You as well." And then Annie went cold all over, for he whispered, "Wish hard for me tonight, Annie, for it's Midsummer's Eve."

"Och, it isnae!" she cried, for she hadn't remembered, and forgetting was like a disloyalty.

"Wish for my sake and Isobel's." he repeated, turning his tawny eyes on her. They looked so pleading that Annie was stunned.

"Aye, I will, all night I will," she answered earnestly, and that seemed to reassure him. Her mind started to whirl. Did he need *her*, then – in the way she needed him for his help and all his sweetness? And could just her wishing help him and Isobel, could it help the time of changing to come? A propeller went round and round in her head, turning her thoughts to foam. She knew that she would wish and hope right fiercely, and there would be little sleep for her that night.

"But can I no' come, Lal, to the fork in the burn?"

Lal shook his head slowly, and his face in the driver's mirror was full of grief.

"You're a close wee thing tonight," Annie's mother said, looking over at her from the sink. Her hands flashed as she sliced chips and flung them into a pan of hot fat.

"I'm tired from the climb," Annie replied, and retired further behind her book.

"You're freckled from being up the hill. What a sight your legs are, too – a' scratches."

Annie froze.

"They *are* scratches, are they no'?"

"Sort of. Cuts from the bracken. I skidded on it."

"Get them washed, though, and some ointment on it."

Annie escaped to the bedroom to find the ointment. Outside the sky was changing, the transparent blue was turning to a heavy, bruised colour. From the window she watched the livid green of the coming storm seep across the valley. The weather was going to break with a vengeance.

Annie's dad arrived late back for tea and bad-tempered from the clammy heat.

"I saw the hydroelectric start up," Annie said tentatively as he soaped his face at the sink. "From the hill, we saw it."

"Och did ye," he spluttered through the suds. "Damn pantomime that was. Talk about looking for the sellotape at the last minute, to get the thing going!" He sluiced his head under the tap and came up slippery and streaming with water. With his eyes tight shut, he went on talking. "As for Rattray-Douglas prancing about in his new kilt, cutting red

76

ribbon – what a carry-on. I fair expected him to bash a bottle of champagne on the thing and launch us all for America." He groped for the towel and rubbed hard. "You could just about hear him jinglin' the compensation in his pockets."

Annie's mother humphed. "He's having them all back at Dal for drinks. I've been polishing that drawing-room floor till ye could eat off it. And the chandelier too. Piece by piece, an hour and a half it took me."

After tea Annie sat by the window to do her homework. She had one eye on the poem in the book, and one eye on the darkening sky. The poem was long and hard and had to be learned under threat of the tawse, by heart. "The curfew tolls the knell of parting day," it went, long swaying lines which made her feel drowsy. She thought sleepily about the Headmaster, and whether he would dare to use the belt now, even if she did get a line wrong. With her cheek against the cool of the window, she dreamed, and her mind wandered away from the poem on to the lines of Isobel's wedding song, and puzzled over them.

"The mother of landslides is heavy-hipped.
The mother of rainbows speaks glory."

She must have nodded off, because her mother's voice woke her with a start.
"You're for your bed, girl."
In her bedroom Annie put a cushion behind her

pillow so that she could lie propped up and see the whole valley through the window. Although midsummer nights were usually light till eleven, the storm had brought the dusk early, and the daylight had almost gone. Craning, she could just see Dal House along the Ridge. Its lights blazed out in the twilight, and she fancied she could see figures dancing behind the mullioned windows. Away down in the valley the eerie blue lights of the dam shone out too.

The first grumble of thunder came from beyond the mountains to the northeast, and sheet lightning flashed over the peaks of Atholl. Annie stared out, with her fingers tight-crossed for Lal, willing and hoping. After a long time in one position, her limbs began to ache. She rubbed them, and settled herself to watch again. Gradually her eyelids sagged, opened with a start, and sagged again. And then the dream – or the vision, she was never quite sure which – came over her.

She saw the man-eagle suspended in the air, and then plunging down into Laggan burn like a gull after herring. Without ripple or splash the bird vanished beneath the surface. And Annie could see into the deep pool by the reeds, see Lal the man embrace a girl whose red hair rippled with the water and whose white skin gleamed slippery as scales. The two of them swam to where the burn met the flooded area by the dam, and Annie saw them come up on to the land where the old halfsubmerged road emerged from the water. She saw them about to disappear round a bend in the road, and panic gripped her, the fear and the knowledge that they would be gone for ever. On the brow of a small hill, by a yellow gorse bush, they paused, and looked back. Her mouth tried to form cries. Come back, she tried to call to them, come back. But they only waved gaily, turned, and were gone.

A clatter of thunder jerked Annie awake. She sat up straight and saw a fork of lightning arrow down on Bohespic Hill. Her fingers ached. They had stayed tight-crossed in her sleep, and she had to rub hard to bring the circulation back. Another bang of thunder came right overhead shaking the windows, and hail began to rattle against the tin roof. Despite the dank heat, she shivered, thinking about her dream. Was it telling the truth, she wondered, with a black misery in her wondering, or was Lal still watching down by the burn with his fingers trailing the water and the rain plastering the shirt to his back.

Just then a huge crash of thunder battered and rolled to and fro across the valley, and a flare of light went up from Bohespic, showering out like a firework display. When the orange flames began to surge up Annie realized that it was no lightning flash, but an explosion.

Her dad was already up and pulling his overalls over his pyjamas.

"What is it, Dad – the fire up the hill?"

"The fuel tanks," he said, and grabbed a rain-coat and a torch. "God knows how they went up."

79

Annie's mother hovered anxiously. "Do ye need to go?"

"They'll need everyone they can get to shift the machines. It'll be a while afore the fire engines come."

"Thank God ye weren't on the night shift."

"It's Ernie's crew the night. I cannae stay here wi' them up there, ye understand."

"Dad, please can I come wi' ye'?" Annie begged. "It's important!"

Her dad looked at her. "This is nae time for silliness, Annie," he said harshly. "You stay with your mother." And he was out of the door and starting up the car engine.

Holding back the tears, Annie went back to her bedroom. She waited quietly in the darkness, while her mother clattered cups in the kitchen.

"Are you sleeping, Annie? Do you want a cup of tea?"

Annie didn't answer. She waited until the kitchen light went out, then she crept through to the hall to get her Wellingtons. Her mother's door was shut, though a light showed underneath it. She pulled on her raincoat and stepped out into the downpour, closing the door softly behind her.

Then she ran and ran, down the boulder-strewn field in front of the house, over fences, marsh and heather. The rain stung her face and soaked the front of her nightgown where her coat flapped open. Cows sheltering in the lee of a dyke lowed out mournfully to her as she raced past. Through the

alder grove she ran, and across the old rigs of
Laggan. Near Laggan the road was busy with the
lights of landrovers and torches, and the noise of
folks shouting, so she kept well out of sight behind
the hedge. The whole valley seemed to be gathered
on the Laggan road – far too many people were
about for her to get to the fork in the burn without
being seen.

Annie sank down behind the hedge to get her
breath back. Up on the hill the fire glowed a soft red
through the rain. Suddenly, as she watched it, the
fire seemed to shudder, as if someone had taken a
great poker and stirred it, and the rumbling
started. Something was happening inside Bohespic
Hill. Something was slipping.

On the other side of the hedge there was a
moment's awed silence, and then a babble of voices.

"Sweet Jesus, is it a landslide, Donny?"

"No, is it?"

"It's the tunnel going."

"Get out of here – the whole hill's goin' tae be
around our heids in a minute."

A siren started to shriek at the dam, and Annie's
blood froze. She peered through the hedge to see if
her dad's car was out there on the road. The
hawthorn tore at her cheek as she scanned the road,
but she could seen no Baby Austin there.

A voice came booming through the megaphone.
"Clear the area. This is a police message. Turn
back. Clear the area."

"But what about the poor souls up the hill?" A

woman's voice protested. "I saw the headlights."

"Clear the area," the megaphone repeated. "This is a danger zone."

Annie cowered behind the dripping hedge. Her mind raced. If only Lal was still at the burn. . . if she cut round behind Laggan, over by the old peat-cuttings, she could get to the fork of the burn. Together they could get her dad off the mountain which was rolling and bucking so restlessly. She jumped up, and, with her head well down, she zigzagged along the hedge and over the fields behind Laggan. Panting hard, she climbed the low ridge where the peat-stacks were.

Up above there was a flash of power lines, and a pylon sagged and fell, silent as a stick insect. Annie hardly glanced at it, so crazy with running was she, so full of the certainty that all she had to do was find Lal and her dad would be safe. Lal would pluck him off the mountain like an apple off a tree, she thought, with a burst of happiness, as she bounded down the ridge towards the burn.

But then she saw the water. A sheet of it, where the ribbon of the burn should have been. The next moment the rest of the water came sweeping round the corner of the ridge, carrying with it half the shoulder of Bohespic — rubble, pipes, fir-trees, struggling sheep.

For a moment Annie stood hypnotized like a rabbit caught in headlights. She stared up at the white and whipping foam on this bank of water which bore down on her, and she thought stupidly that it was like suds, soapsuds on her dad's neck.

And then she was back to her senses and racing up the valley, heading for higher ground. The spray hit her first, like a slap, then a tumbling fence post swept her legs from under her. And then she too was flotsam in the dark stew of the current, with foxes and dead trees for company. Her last memory, before blackness took her, was of reaching out for a branch, and closing her fingers around the antlers of a terrified deer.

* * *

Annie woke with an itch at her neck and a bright light in her eyes. She moved her arm to push the scratchy blanket away from her chin and winced with pain.

"Nurse! She's come round." Her dad's face bent over her. "You're all right now, lass, you're fine now."

Her mother's face came into focus too, her eyes red with weeping. She put a handkerchief to her mouth and muttered, "Thank God."

"Dad wasnae in the landslide?" Annie mumbled, with difficulty, through sore lips.

"No, no, I never got through the roadblock. . . but you wheesht now. Rest yourself."

"Where's this?" Annie craned to see, but found

she was strapped down.

"It's the ambulance to Pitlochry. We won't be long now."

A nurse with very clean fingernails bent over and took Annie's pulse. Her touch was soft and cool. "We just have to X-ray you to see if anything's broken," she said cheerily. "We think you're just bruised, really."

At the hospital the staff were stretched to the limit with all the cases of shock and concussion coming in from Laggan. In Casualty the doctor's hands fluttered over her quick as sparrows, then she was wheeled off to the X-ray room. Eventually a nurse gave her sweet tea and a biscuit and joked about the rare colours her bruises would be in the morning, and she was pronounced well enough to go home. Her dad wrapped her in a tartan rug and carried her to the back seat of the Baby Austin, where, stiff but cosy, she fell fast asleep.

* * *

She woke in her own bed, with the sun high over the valley. Gingerly she eased herself up on her pillows to see out of the window.

The valley was a glittering sheet of water, dotted with floating trees. The rooftops of Laggan were gone for ever, and the old road disappeared, and the peat-diggings. Only the high ridge of Dal was left above the surface. And over the highest point of the ridge, where the Grey Dancer swayed tall and proud at the top of the birch wood, a new rainbow arched.

Through her open window Annie could hear the hens scrabbling in the yard, and her mother's voice talking to Alec the postie.

"Thank God, our Annie's going to be all right," she was saying.

"It's a miracle it was only two that lost their lives," Alec said. "They're still dragging the flood for the bodies, though."

"Ssh," her mother warned, and Annie strained to hear her next words. "A terrible thing about the Dominie," she whispered. Annie crept out of bed and hid behind the curtains.

"Aye," Alec said in a low voice, "makes ye wonder what he was doing hanging round there. He was found near the dam, an awful sight, I heard. They dragged him out from under half a ton of rock – what was left of the poor soul."

Annie felt a wave of sickness come over her, and she clung to the windowsill.

"A very terrible thing," her mother muttered below. "And when I think Will might have been up that hill – I cannae bear to think on it. He just says well, his number wasnae up yet, and it's fate."

Annie's stomach cramped with nausea as the memories flooded back. "Mam," she cried out, "Mam!"

"Och, she's been listening," her mother said, and hurried upstairs. She came into the bedroom with her arms full of washing.

"Who rescued me?" Annie cried. "Who pulled me out?"

"Why, it was Lachlan McLellan, of course! Did your dad no say?"

Annie shook her head numbly.

"Back to bed now," her mother fussed, dropping the washing on a chair and straightening the pillows. "That's a brave man for you," she went on. "From what I hear yours wasnae the only life he saved. There's many folks will be thanking him today."

Annie lay back on her pillows, weak with tiredness and relief. The churning in her stomach began to subside.

"Where's Dad?" she asked after a while.

"He's down by the flood. They're clearing the mud with bulldozers. It's an awful mess down there."

By evening Annie felt nearly herself again, and wanted to get up for tea, but her mother insisted she stay in bed. She was just finishing her broth when her dad came in. His overalls were stained with mud and oil, but he gave her a hug regardless.

"How's the invalid, then?" he asked cheerily, but his face was white and worried. "Ye've some roses back in that peaky face again."

"Dad," Annie said excitedly, "Dad – Lal saved me, didn't he?"

"Aye." Her dad turned away and patted his overall pockets, searching for cigarettes.

"Well?" said Annie.

"Well what?"

Alarm began to prickle between Annie's shoulder blades. Something was wrong. "Well when can I see him? I've got to say thank you, have I no'?"

Her dad's hand shook as he held a match to his cigarette. He reached out and took Annie's hand. "Be brave now, lass. It's bad news. Your friend's dead. They found him this afternoon."

"In the water?" Annie said, disbelieving.

"Aye. And the girl as well. The one that helped him bring you to the shore. A girl not from these parts. In a queer green gown."

"No, no. I dinnae believe you. It isn't true!" Annie screamed out, and toppled her broth on to the floor. "They're no gone, they cannae be gone away!" A terrible desolation spread through her, a pain too keen to bear which turned the room to the colour of lead. Her dad sat and rocked her as the news came swinging at her again and again, like a pendulum each time lashing up a fury of grief. Dimly she heard her mother say, "Gie her these, Will, the doctor left them just in case."

And then, mercifully, she was being lulled away into sleep by the soft movements of a rowboat. Her dad was at the oars, and the boat rocked gently with each eddy in the river current.

It was two weeks before Annie was strong enough to go back to school. Day by day, as the flood waters ebbed, her grief eased a bit, until now it had changed to a dull, consistent ache. Her mother had wanted to keep her off longer, but Annie had pleaded, saying she was bored, and needed something to occupy her mind, even lessons.

The Headmaster's funeral had been and gone, and Black Alistair lay in the graveyard next to his mother, under a big carnation wreath which said: 'From all the pupils of Crianoch school.'

Since it was so near the end of term, no new teacher had come to take his place. Miss Boyd ran the school single-handed, counting on the older pupils to get on with their work by themselves. Although the shadow of Black Alistair's death still lay over the school, it was a calmer and freer place altogether, and Annie was not the only one to feel that, she could tell from the smiles and the murmurs in class and the way Ian Blain looked dreamily out of the window instead of twitching like a snared badger.

At dinner-time that day Annie felt Lal's house tugging at her, as she had known it would. She didn't stop to argue with herself, but slipped out of the playground without even thinking up an excuse, and ran down the brae to the Co-op.

The door swung open to a fingertip's pressure. Annie walked in, holding her breath. The paint glowed whiter now that the room had been emptied of furniture. The drawing was gone from the wall, and the rich rug from the floor. A birch broom stood forlornly in the corner, guarding a pile of dust.

And then Annie's breath came whistling out in a long sigh. On the mantelpiece was a sheet of paper, rolled up like a scroll. In one bound Annie was across the room. When she unrolled the paper the white knife slid out into her hand, and she looked down at the drawing of the Grey Dancer.

Annie held the knife in the palm of her hand and watched her tears blur the shining blade.

A small wind came through the room then, stirring the pile of dust. And in her head, it was as if the wind set up a rustling, like the shiver of reeds at the loch's edge. And in the whispering she seemed to hear, faint but clear enough, the words:

"We leave you the knife for truth, and for the fight."

Annie stood there an age in the white room, until the weeping stopped, and with it the twisting in her heart.

Then, slipping the knife into the pocket of her dress, she walked out into the sunshine and closed the door firmly behind her.

When Marnie Was There

JOAN G. ROBINSON

Brooding, lonely Anna, a foster-child, goes to stay with a kind Norfolk couple. There, like something in her memory, she finds the old house backing on to the creek. But it is the girl at the window who haunts her . . . Marnie, headstrong, often infuriating and somehow just as elusive when the two meet as she had been at the window. Marnie becomes Anna's perfect friend, and though she finally vanishes for good, she has helped Anna to make real friends.

This is a thrilling, intense story, part mystery, part adventure, part fantasy, and will appeal particularly to girls of eleven and upward.

THE CHRONICLES OF NARNIA
C. S. Lewis

C. S. Lewis's wit and wisdom, his blend of excitement and adventure with fantasy, have made this magnificent series beloved of many generations of readers. The final book, *The Last Battle*, won the Carnegie Medal for 1956.

Each of the seven titles is a complete story in itself, but all take place in the magical land of Narnia. Guided by the noble Lion, Aslan, the children learn that evil and treachery can only be overcome by courage, loyalty and great sacrifice.

The titles, in suggested reading order, are as follows:

The Magician's Nephew
The Lion, the Witch and the Wardrobe
The Horse and his Boy
Prince Caspian
The Voyage of the Dawn Treader
The Silver Chair
The Last Battle

THE SILVER CROWN

Robert O'Brien

'She did not know how late it was, nor how long she had
been asleep, when she was awakened by a loud squealing of
brakes, a long and frightening screech of tyres. The car
stopped so abruptly that she was thrown forward and hit her
head on the button that snaps the glove compartment shut...
Ellen saw lying inside a pistol with a long barrel she recog-
nized instantly, and a shimmering green hood with two eye-
holes staring vacantly up at her.'

Fear gripped Ellen. Who was this Mr Gates? Why had he
been so keen to give her a lift? And was that the green hood
the robber had worn? This was only the start of her long
journey, in which the silver crown played a mysterious part.

'No doubt about the impact of this strange, eerie, absorbing
book.'

Naomi Lewis

The Eyes of the Amaryllis
NATALIE BABBITT

When, in 1850, the brig *Amaryllis* was swallowed in a hurricane, the captain and all the crew were swallowed too. Thirty years later Geneva Reade, the captain's ageing widow, was still waiting, certain that her husband would send her a message from the bottom of the sea. Each and every high tide she combed the beach, watched by a sad, mysterious man she called Seward, although she had known him by another name in happier days, before the *Amaryllis* was lost.

Into this weird and haunted situation comes Jenny, the widow's granddaughter, and the three of them are drawn into a kind of deadly game with each other and the sea. A game that only the sea knows how to win.

The Eyes of the Amaryllis is a moving and engrossing story, simply and beautifully written.

The Mountain of Magic

BEVERLEY NICHOLS

The battle between good and evil began in *The Tree That Sat Down* and *The Stream That Stood Still* comes to a dramatic climax in the final volume of Beverley Nichols' fantasy trilogy. Jill and her brother Jack set out on an expedition to the mountain of magic and are pursued by Sam and the witch Miss Smith, who are determined to get their final revenge and destroy the children.

Beverley Nichols' woodland fantasy trilogy will enchant readers of nine up.

The Tree That Sat Down and *The Stream That Stood Still* are also available in Lions.

Private, Keep Out!
GWEN GRANT

I have written a book. It's all about the street we live on – me and our Mam and Dad, and our Pete and Tone, and Lucy, Rose and Joe. They're my brothers and sisters, worst luck.

I don't see why I should be nice to that stuck-up dancing teacher Miss Brown just because Pete's going to marry her, and how *can* you tell if angels are really men or women?

Growing up in a north-east Midlands colliery town just after the War, the narrator, youngest in a family of six, is never out of trouble. She is high-spirited, impulsive, stubborn and often exasperated by her parents and older brothers and sisters, but she will win the heart of every reader in her determined efforts to keep her end up.